This igloo book belongs to:

.................................................................

# igloobooks

Published in 2019
by Igloo Books Ltd
Cottage Farm
Sywell
NN6 0BJ
www.igloobooks.com

0819 001.01
2 4 6 8 10 9 7 5 3 1
ISBN 978-1-78905-425-5

Written by Stephanie Moss
Illustrated by Katya Longhi

Designed by Justine Ablett
Edited by Stephanie Moss

Printed and manufactured in China

# Christmas Llama

igloobooks

The llamas lived up high
where it was sunny all day long.
But Lucy wasn't happy.
She just felt something was wrong.

She hated trekking up the hills
out in the blazing sun.
Their fancy clothes were itchy
and she wasn't having fun!

She dreamed of cosy scarves and playing in the snow all day.

And what Lucy really wanted was to help pull Santa's sleigh!

Season's Greetings

GIFTS IN STORE NOW!

**"That job is just for reindeer!"** Lucy's llama friends all cried.

But nothing changed her mind. It didn't matter how they tried.

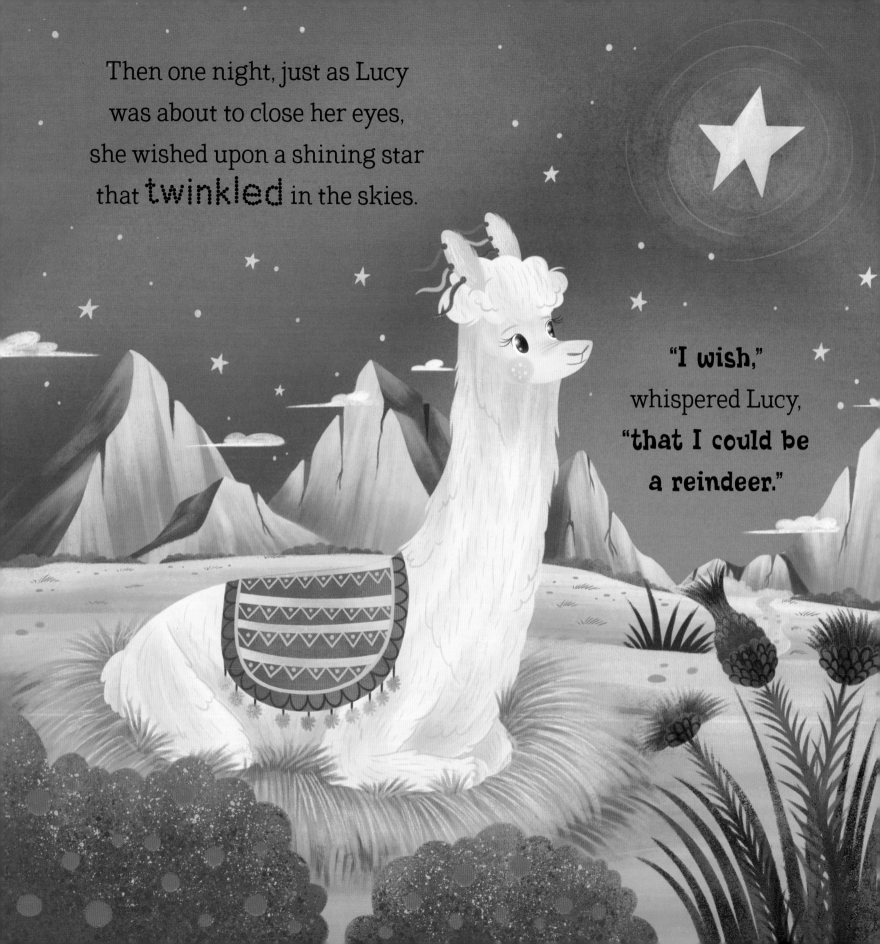

Then one night, just as Lucy was about to close her eyes, she wished upon a shining star that **twinkled** in the skies.

"I wish," whispered Lucy, "that I could be a reindeer."

And before she knew it...
she saw Santa's sleigh appear!

"**Ho-ho-ho!**" cried Santa.

"**Lucy, thank goodness you're here.
My reindeer all have Christmas Pox
and can't help me this year.**"

Santa said the reindeer needed somewhere warm to rest,
so he'd need a replacement, and that Lucy passed the test!

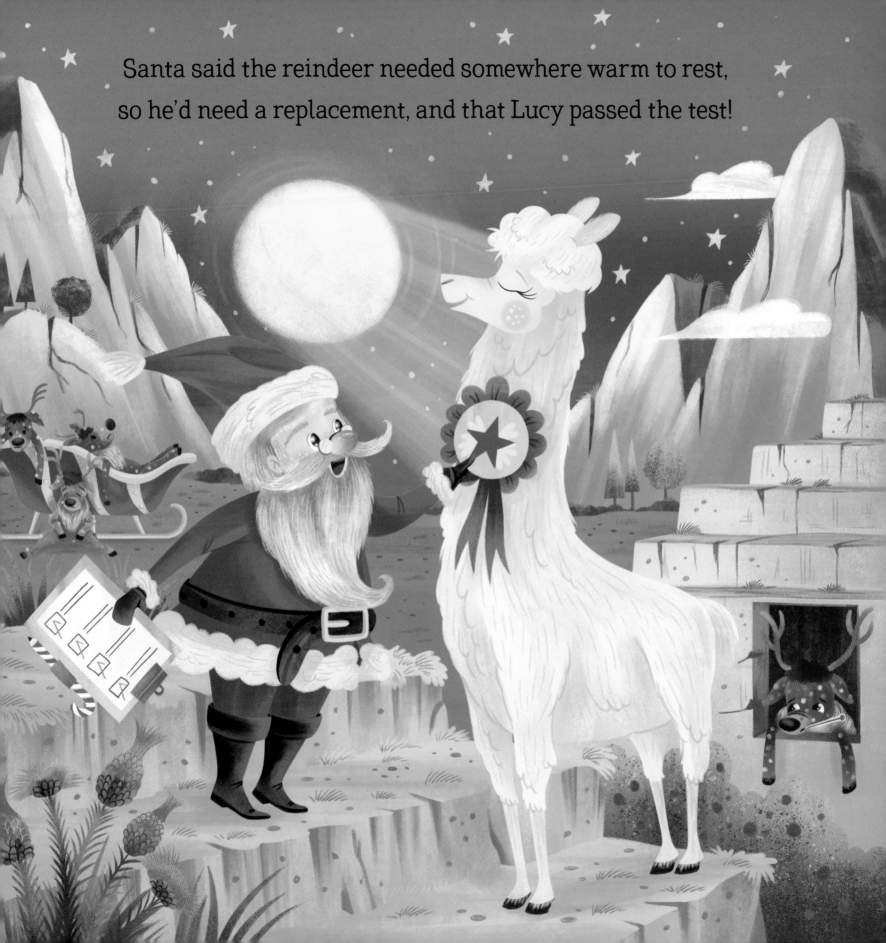

"You carry heavy loads," said Santa, "up and down all day. I'll sprinkle you with magic dust and we'll be on our way!"

Lucy was amazed that
all her dreams were coming true.
Then Santa slipped her reins on
and she knew just what to do.

Lucy pulled the heavy sleigh around the world with ease.

Its bells jingled around her as snowflakes danced on the breeze.

The gifts were soon delivered. **"To the North Pole!"** Santa cried.

They landed by the workshop and the elves were Lucy's guide.

They went sledging in the snow. She wore cute Christmas pyjamas.
They even found four Christmas socks made specially for llamas!

"**Have this cocoa with marshmallows,**" they said, "**and this Christmas hat.**"
They made snowmen.
They had snowball fights.
"**Hey, watch out, Lucy!**"

Splat!

"Bye, Lucy!" the elves all cried,
when it was time to leave.
"Please come back and visit,
if you're free next
Christmas Eve?"

But when Santa took her home,
can you guess what they saw there?
The reindeer were all better, and
were lounging on deckchairs!

"It's time to go," said Santa,
but one reindeer shook her head.
"The North Pole is so cold!" she cried.
"We're staying here instead."

Lucy smiled and said, **"I dreamed of leaving my home, too. But after my adventure, I know just what will help you!"**

Lucy helped them bring the best of both their worlds together.
For Christmas is for everyone, no matter what the weather!

From then on, Lucy Llama always spread her festive cheer.
She had finally achieved her dream of being a reindeer.

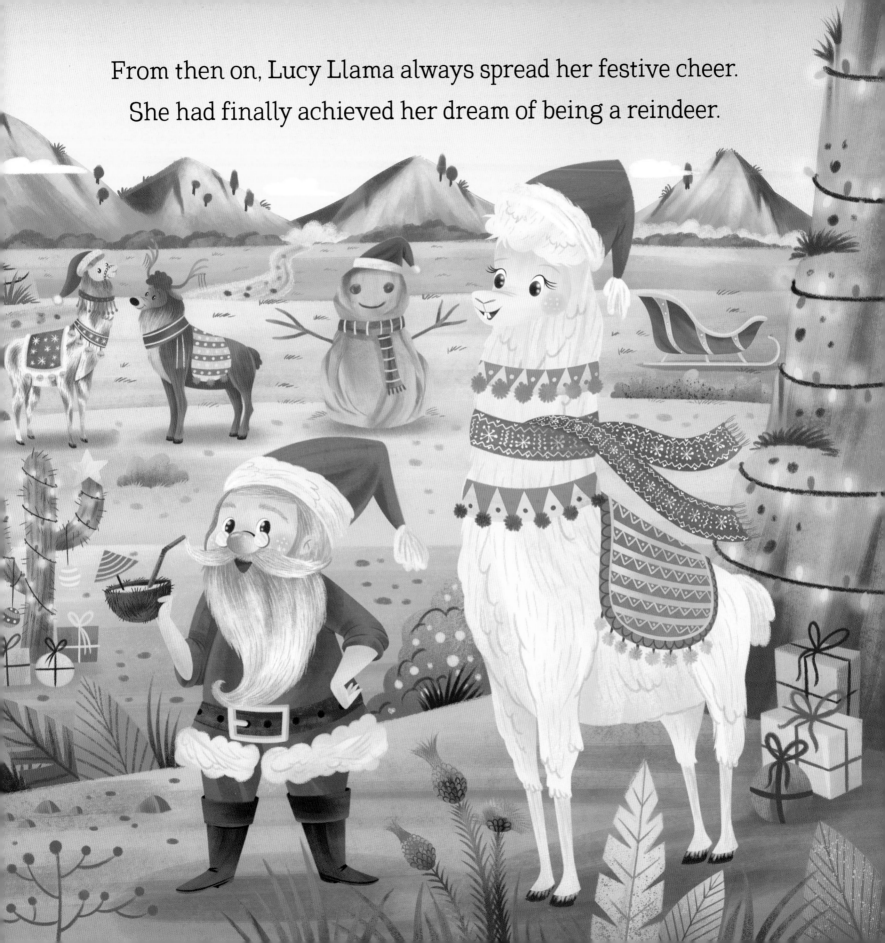